Nat the Cat

CAN SLEEP LIKE THAT

Words by Victoria Allenby

Illustrations by Tara Anderson

pajamapress

First Paperback Edition Published in 2014
Text copyright © Victoria Allenby
Illustration copyright © Tara Anderson
This edition copyright © 2013 Pajama Press

10 9 8 7 6 5 4 3 2

Canada Council   Conseil des arts
for the Arts   du Canada

ONTARIO ARTS COUNCIL
CONSEIL DES ARTS DE L'ONTARIO
an Ontario government agency
un organisme du gouvernement de l'Ontario

The publisher gratefully acknowledges the support of the Canada Council for the Arts and the Ontario Arts Council for its publishing program. We acknowledge the financial support of the Government of Canada through the Book Publishing Industry Development Program (BPIDP) for our publishing activities.

Library and Archives Canada Cataloguing in Publication

Allenby, Victoria, 1989-, author
Nat the cat can sleep like that / Victoria Allenby ; illustrated by Tara Anderson.
For children ages 2-6. ISBN 978-1-927485-70-5

I. Anderson, Tara, illustrator II. Title.

PS8601.L44658N38 2013   jC813'.6   C2013-902731-9

Publisher Cataloging-in-Publication Data (U.S.)

Allenby, Victoria, 1989-
    Nat the cat can sleep like that / Victoria Allenby ; Tara Anderson.
[32] p. : col. ill. ;   cm.
Summary: Nat the cat can sleep in, on, under, and around anything—but can he sleep through the antics of a rambunctious kitten?
ISBN-13: 978-1-927485-70-5

1. Cats – Juvenile fiction. 2. Humorous stories – Juvenile literature. 3. Bedtime – Juvenile fiction.
I. Anderson, Tara, 1974- . II. Title.
[E] dc23   PZ7.A453Na 2013

JUV002050 JUVENILE FICTION / Animals / Cats
JUV019000 JUVENILE FICTION / Humorous Stories
JUV057000 JUVENILE FICTION / Stories in Verse
JUV010000 JUVENILE FICTION / Bedtime & Dreams

Manufactured by Sheck Wah Tong Printing Ltd.
Printed in China

Pajama Press Inc.
181 Carlaw Ave. Suite 207, Toronto, Ontario, Canada
www.pajamapress.ca

Printed especially for The Learning Partnership's Welcome to Kindergarten™ program.

The Learning
Partnership
PUBLIC EDUCATION. CANADA'S FUTURE.

www.thelearningpartnership.ca

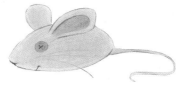

The original art is rendered in mixed media using Prismacolor pencil crayon, watercolor, gouache, acrylic paint, and glaze on 300-pound hot press Fabriano watercolor paper.

For my mother, who loves words too
—V.A.

For my mom, who loves cats;
for Sasha, the kitten who stole everyone's hearts;
and for Tigger, who inspired me to draw cats in the first place
—T.A.

Morning comes with hum and hurry,
Clatter, patter, scramble, scurry.
Running feet and banging door,

Honking—
Wait! Is that a snore?
Who could sleep through all of that?

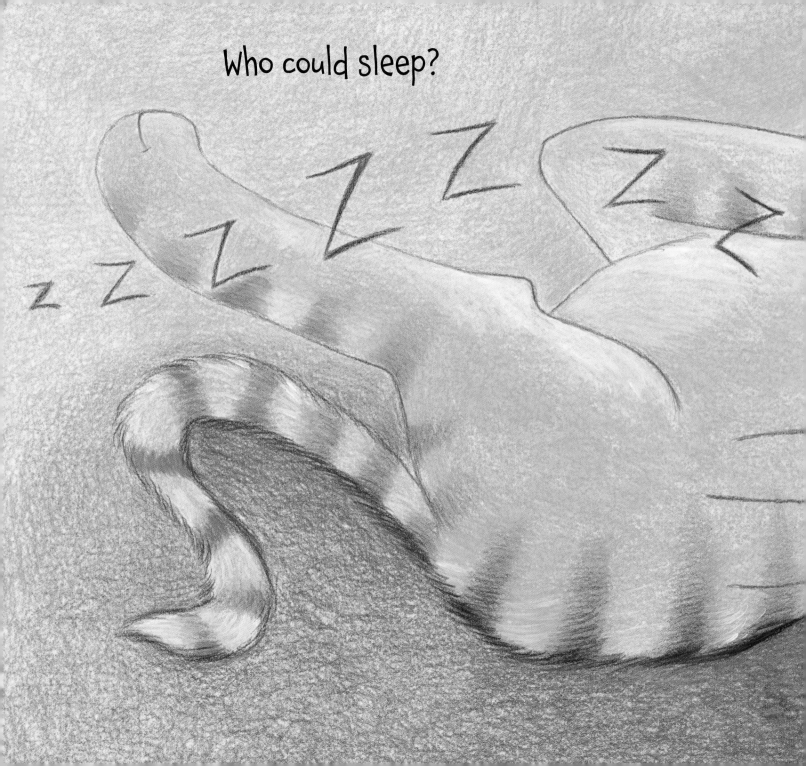

Nat can sleep in dresser drawers,

Or in front of bedroom doors.

under blankets, on a stair,

upside-down on someone's chair—
Nat the cat can sleep like that!

In a basket safe and snug,

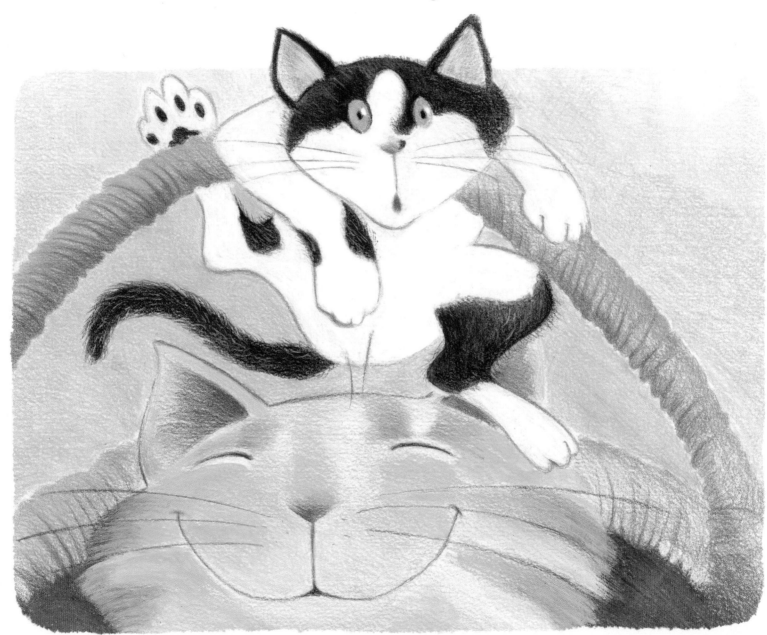

Or where sunbeams warm the rug,

Curled inside a cooking pot,

Hidden in a secret spot—
Nat the cat can sleep like that!

Flopping halfway off a shelf,

Folded over on himself,

With his paws all tucked inside,

Or with limbs flung open wide—
Nat the cat can sleep like that!

BUT

When the lights are all turned out,
When there's no one else about,

When the nighttime quiet falls,

When strange shadows fill the halls,

When the wind is WHOOSHH
and SHUSHH

When the darkness murmurs, HUSH!

When the house is wrapped in dreams,

When stars wink and moonlight gleams,

Nat the cat can't ever... ever... ever...

Sleep through that!